Sugar F

Reginald Bretnor

Alpha Editions

This edition published in 2024

ISBN : 9789364738910

Design and Setting By
Alpha Editions
www.alphaedis.com
Email - info@alphaedis.com

As per information held with us this book is in Public Domain.
This book is a reproduction of an important historical work. Alpha Editions uses the best technology to reproduce historical work in the same manner it was first published to preserve its original nature. Any marks or number seen are left intentionally to preserve its true form.

Sugar Plum

By R. BRETNOR

Illustrated by ASHMAN

If not for two items, this would be a funny story—the Atomic Age brought back the 1925 vogue, and inhibition is not shatter-proof.

On a clear spring evening in 2189, Charles Edward Button came home half an hour late for his supper, tossed his hat to the robot butler who came out from behind the DoItAll, and announced that he had just bought a planet.

His wife, Betty, was looking small and long-suffering on a plastic reproduction of a Victorian love-seat, and her cousin Aurelia, a large, handsome woman, was standing behind her protectively.

"Of course," he informed them, "it's not a *big* planet. But what a bargain! With real oceans, and two moons, and—"

"Real estate, real estate, real estate!" Cousin Aurelia's tart voice cut him off in mid-sentence. "You know what's come of every one of your investments. Call the man *right now* and tell him you want your money back!"

"I'm afraid it's too late." Charles avoided her eye. "I bought it up at a tax-auction and—well, the government never refunds."

"I *thought* so. A planet nobody wants. Probably all run down, with swamps and deserts, and in some dreadful, shabby district where the neighbors have squirmy tentacles, or eyes on stalks, or big, nasty beaks!"

"It isn't at all. It's in a good neighborhood—only two systems away from the Inchcapes' new summer planet. A little remote, but that means more privacy." He took a catalogue out of his pocket. "'Parcel 71,'" he read.

"'Sugar Plum, a Class IV planet'—that means it's like Earth, only bigger—'claimed 8/12/85 by Space Captain Alexander Burgee, under Planetary Homestead Act of 2147 (amended.)' And here's his description of the place where he landed: 'Neat as a pin, fine climate, full of critters and fish, quite uninhabited.' He was lost in Deep Space, poor fellow. That's why they sold it."

Betty smiled faintly. "The Inchcapes call their planet Bide-A-Wee. I think Sugar Plum's ever so much nicer. But—but can we afford it?"

"We certainly can't!" fumed Cousin Aurelia. "We'll put it back on the market and salvage whatever we can."

"No, we won't," Charles said firmly. "And it's not just a summer resort. We're pulling up stakes to live there all year round."

Betty gasped.

Cousin Aurelia straightened up, bristling.

"I have made up my mind," Charles went on. "I have done a lot of serious thinking." He pointed at the heavily framed neo-daguerreotype portraits on the walls. "Our ancestors rediscovered the only *true* principles, those of the great Nineteenth Century. They brought the Second Victorian Age into being. Civilization reached its peak, its full flowering. But now all is crumbling before the poisonous onslaught of modernism. We who have not been corrupted must seek out a refuge. That, Cousin, is why I bought Sugar Plum."

"Nonsense!" exclaimed Cousin Aurelia. "There may be changes everywhere else, but never in Boston."

"Ha!" Charles looked at his watch. "Solomon!" he called out.

The butler came bowing out of the DoItAll nook, where the servants stayed when they were switched off. He wore a swallowtail coat and knee-breeches, and had kinky white hair. Made to order, he was Cousin Aurelia's idea.

"Yassuh, Marse Charles. Here Ah is."

"Solomon," ordered Charles, "tune in Watson Widgett."

Betty paled, uttering a polite little scream.

"Are you *mad*?" cried Cousin Aurelia. "I've heard about him. I'll not have that man in *my* home!"

Charles squared his shoulders. "Cousin, may I remind you that *I* am head of this house, and that we are *Victorians*? It's high time you found out what's going on. Solomon!"

"Yass*uh*."

There was a click from the DoItAll, a brief flash of light and a figure appeared in their midst, a cheerful young man in loose trousers and shirt, without coat, waistcoat, cravat, or even a pair of suspenders. He was grinning at Cousin Aurelia.

"Boys and girls," he was saying, "Wyoming has outlawed corsets! The folks in Siskiyou, California, have given women the vote! And listen to this. The Bikini swimsuit—just a wisp and a twist—is back on the market!" He winked loathsomely. "Yes, indeed, our prize fake Victorians, our second-hand stuffed shirts, are due for a fall. Here's the best news today, from a cute little lady right here in old Boston." He unfolded a paper. "Dear Watsy, When I first found your program, I was a real Mrs. Biedermeyer. Marriage was something we gentlewomen tried to endure while we knitted an anti-macassar. It wasn't supposed to be fun. Then a friend tipped me off to your—"

At this point, Cousin Aurelia emitted a shriek, rolled her eyes and crumpled to the carpet.

Charles gestured and the commentator vanished with a click and a flash. Betty scurried out and returned with the smelling salts.

Presently, Cousin Aurelia regained her senses, shivered, and said, "It's too awful for words. If it were not for Betty, I would surely have left long ago. As it is, I shall go where you go, to protect her, of course."

Then she permitted Betty to help her to her feet and out of the room.

"Solomon!" Charles called loudly.

"Yassuh, Marse Charles."

"Set the table for two," Charles commanded. "I shall dial the dinner myself."

He felt very adventurous and masterful. Dialing dinner without aid was fine training in self-reliance.

Six weeks later, the three of them stood on the bridge of the space freighter *Beautiful Joe*, watching Sugar Plum as the vessel entered an orbit around it.

But Charles Edward Button didn't feel at all masterful, or even adventurous.

They stood next to Possett, the skipper, a great, hairy man with gold teeth, a bad squint, and an air of gloomy cunning about him. After her first look at Possett, Cousin Aurelia had locked herself in her cabin, allowing no one but Betty to approach her, and threatening to subsist on the half-dozen cases of Dr. Stringfellow's Vegetable Remedy she kept under her berth.

Charles, however, had been sure that Possett's heart was both kindly and chivalrous.

"Take those tall stories of his," he said more than once. "Betty, they don't mean a thing. Old spacedogs love to kid tenderfeet. Imagine trying to make me believe that it's dangerous out here! And all that malarkey about Captain Burgee being a pirate or something!"

They stared at Sugar Plum, at its small polar ice caps, its seas, its continents greener than Earth's, its wandering white clouds. Not many hours before, it had been only a dust mote, a pinpoint of light in the void. Now it filled half the sky. And suddenly Charles understood the immensities, the unspeakable stretches of space in which Boston had vanished.

Shivering, he wished he were home, stiffly safe in a curlicued chair, with Solomon dialing his dinner for him.

"Nice piece of property," grunted Possett around his cigar. "Too bad about—" He broke off with a shrug.

"About what?" asked Charles, alarmed.

"I wouldn't want to be in your shoes if Burgee comes around and finds you'd run off with his planet."

"Burgee? He was lost out in space!"

"His kind don't stay lost. Chances are he's hiding out from the law. But it's none of my business. Just thought I'd warn you."

Charles laughed weakly. "You c-can't frighten me. I'm sure there aren't any pirates in space any more."

Possett turned to his weasel-faced mate. "Loopy, call the New Texas spaceport. Get Mac on the screen."

The mate nodded. He twiddled a dial and punched at a switch. The screen glowed. After some seconds, the face of a red-haired person appeared, looking rather disgusted.

"New Texas, New Texas," came a voice. "I hear you, *Beautiful Joe*. What the hell do you want?"

"Dude aboard wants some info," said Possett. "Wants to know what Burgee did for a living—Alexander Burgee. Also, are the coppers still trying to find him?"

The face frowned. "Possett, you know damn well Burgee was a pirate. You know he's been listed as lost. Now quit wasting my time. New Texas out."

The face vanished. The mate snickered nastily. And Charles just stood there gaping.

"A real pirate!" squeaked Cousin Aurelia. "Wh-what would he do? Would he *kill* us?"

"Might do anything. But—" eying her, Possett leered—"he's like me. Likes 'em well fattened up. Lady, you needn't worry."

Cousin Aurelia paled. She started to sway. Then, perhaps recalling the uncarpeted deck, she recovered and looked haughty instead.

"I am going right back to my cabin," she proclaimed, and stalked off the bridge.

"Cousin Aurelia is very genteel," Betty snapped at the captain. "You had no right to insult her. Besides, she's only twenty pounds overweight."

"Don't mind me. I go for her type." Possett shook his head darkly and turned toward Charles. "Button, man to man, a back-country planet's no place for the ladies. Look, I'll take the thing off your hands. I can handle Burgee. Twelve thousand cold cash for your stuff and the deed, and I'll throw in a lift to New Texas. There's a liner from there."

Charles thought of the comfortable Earth and was tempted. "But I paid thirty-five," he protested uncertainly. "I mean, twelve is—"

"Take it or leave it. I'm trying to do you a favor."

"No, I guess we'll leave it," answered Betty.

Charles looked around in surprise. Her lips were compressed, her blue eyes narrowed with astonishing determination.

"We've come all this way," she declared, "so we might as well keep it. I think it has—well, possibilities. We've had the whole house done over and the servants remodeled. And we'll have all the DoItAll services—teleprojection, medical care, and everything else—from the New Texas substation. I'm sure we'll get along nicely."

The skipper of the *Beautiful Joe* wasn't pleased. "It's your necks. Don't be blaming me for what happens," he growled. "Well, where do you want to set down?"

"Set down?" gulped Charles. "R-right now?"

"Land and unload, it says in the contract. I ain't got all day. I'll dump you at Burgee's old landing, load up with fresh water, and blast off for New Texas."

Charles had no other spot in mind.

"Okay," Possett said to the two robot crewmen at the main controls, "take her down."

At the waterfall's edge, flowering trees twisted their roots in the cliffside, and a fresh wind scattered plumes of its spray through their leaves. Taller trees, bell-blossomed, fanned out from the pool, gave way to a meadow, and followed the course of the stream down a broadening valley—among faceted boulders of translucent quartz, rose-pink, green, and golden, sheltering small, lustrous spires of fragile fungi.

On the meadow stood the house, the latest in Second Victorian, complete with carved plastic false-front in early Schenectady Gothic. The Buttons themselves, with Cousin Aurelia, stood in front of it. They wore long linen dusters and sun helmets with heavy mosquito veils. They were going exploring.

Cousin Aurelia was sputtering: "Do you know what he said when he left? 'Kid, you come along with Mike Possett. You don't want no part of that planet. I'll show you a ripsnorting time!' Then he gave me a look that—that was positively *lecherous*." She shuddered. "At least we'll have no more of that nonsense. Your planet is uninhabited."

Betty looked worried. "I've the funniest feeling," she said. "As if someone was watching."

"That's absurd!" snapped Cousin Aurelia. "You must be imagin—" She stopped in her tracks. "Wh-what's *that*?"

They looked. A large, soft, fuzzy beast had come out from under the trees. It was reddish and had very big feet. It blinked at them brightly, climbed a transparent green rock, and started to whistle, not too tunefully, through its long Roman nose.

Almost instantly, another emerged, a size smaller. Lowering its eyelids coquettishly, it began clapping its forepaws.

"Charles, they must be the 'critters' Burgee mentioned in that catalogue. Remember? I'm sure they're perfectly harmless."

Two more animals appeared and made for a rock of their own. And then there were, suddenly, dozens—all around the edge of the meadow. These were petite, creamy, with lavender ears. They came bounding forward in pairs, sat up and regarded the Buttons solemnly.

Charles began to relax. Somehow, Sugar Plum didn't seem half so enormous any longer, now that they weren't so alone.

"I wonder if they could be tamed." Betty was wistful.

"They're certain to be just full of fleas," sniffed Cousin Aurelia.

The creatures were playful. As the Buttons walked over the meadow, they frolicked around them—

But they also were very affectionate. As they frolicked, they flirted. Every once in a while, each pair would pause to rub noses, to murmur seductively, to nip one another.

At first, Cousin Aurelia tried to pretend they weren't there. But finally she halted. "Charles Edward Button, I won't go a step farther till you drive those nasty things away. It's disgraceful. They're apt to do—anything!"

Charles flushed under his netting. "Shoo!" he said ineffectively. "Beat it!"

There was a swift patter of feet straight ahead and a figure flashed into view. She was slim. She was small, with a girdle and headdress of feathers. Her skin was sky-blue, and her ears were pointed, and her eyes were simply enormous. But she looked distressingly human.

In an instant, she vanished. As the Buttons stood there goggling, they heard more running footsteps, somewhat heavier, and a scuffle, a giggle, a clear, tenor laugh, and then silence.

"Why, that was a girl!" Betty gasped.

"She was being pursued!" Charles exclaimed. "He—he caught her!"

"Oooh!" moaned Cousin Aurelia, covering her eyes. "Charles, how *could* you? Enticing us here, saying it was uninhabited!"

Then, before Charles could find a reply:

"Unin*hab*ited?" chuckled a deep male voice right behind them. "It certainly isn't. It's just unin*hib*ited!"

Slowly, the Buttons turned around. There, by an odd square tree, stood a man even bigger than Possett, smoking a pipe. He was middle-aged. He wore a heavy brown beard, khaki shorts, a deep coat of tan, and a self-possessed smile.

He bowed. "Burgee is my name—Space Captain Alexander Burgee. Glad to make your acquaintance."

"It's him!" screamed Cousin Aurelia. "And he's practically naked!" She pointed a cotton-gloved finger, began backing away. "You fiend, don't you come any nearer. Don't you *touch* me!"

The captain looked very surprised. "Why would I want to?"

Her voice reached a new high and clung there. "You—you libertine! You may lead a riotous life with these natives, but you won't work your will on me. I'll lock myself in till the police can come from New Texas!"

And, tripping and stumbling over her duster, she fled.

As the door banged behind her, the captain nudged a large beast off a nearby rock, and sat down. "I can see that Earth hasn't changed," he remarked. "You tourists still seem to have the daffiest notions." He sounded quite hurt. "Look, these natives are nice little people. They're harmless. I call 'em my Sugar Plum pixies, and sometimes we grin at each other. But that's all. They aren't much past the animal stage. Besides, they lay eggs. Oh, well—" he shrugged as the Buttons exchanged knowing looks—"I have plenty of room at the house and I guess you'll be permanent guests, so welcome to Sugar Plum, anyway."

Betty said angrily, "Sugar Plum's ours. You didn't pay taxes and they sold it at auction. Charles has the deed in his pocket."

"You poor, dumb kids!" The captain seemed really concerned. "You bought some fool bureaucrats error. I'm paid up in advance. Come on down, you can see the receipt."

"Aren't you clever?" said Betty scornfully. "Well, you won't trap us as easily as that. We don't need you or your house."

"You just might want something to eat, or a hot, soapy shower, or a tight roof over you when it rains."

The Buttons smiled triumphantly. They had their own house, with a DoItAll to do everything for them.

"You can leave us alone, Mr. Pirate Burgee. Captain Possett told us your whole horrible story, and Cousin Aurelia is calling the police right this minute."

"Possett?" The captain's face twitched. "Mike Possett, of the *Beautiful Joe*?"

"That's right." Charles felt very superior. "Now you beat it before—"

He didn't finish. From the house came a loud, anguished cry.

They whirled.

Cousin Aurelia, disheveled without helmet or duster, was almost upon them.

"Charles! It won't work!"

She reached him, threw her arms round his neck and hung on.

"I can't turn the servants on, or the teleprojection, or even the keys to the closets. Oh, Charles, we'll have nothing to eat, or to drink, or to wear!"

"That's impossible. DoItAlls never break down."

"We can't live without it!" screeched Cousin Aurelia. "We're millions of miles from Boston! We're marooned with that monster!"

Burgee's long, low house was indecently plain, without even so much as a gimcrack or bit of gingerbread decoration. Its many wide windows looked out over a lake set with islands. Its living room had broad, cushioned couches and indolent chairs—all suspiciously comfortable.

In exactly such houses, Charles knew, in the wicked old days, a fate worse than death had been practically part of the fixtures.

"We shouldn't have let him persuade us," he worriedly told Betty. "Perhaps we'd have starved, but at least Cousin Aurelia wouldn't have locked herself alone into a strange pirate's bedroom!"

"We've been here all afternoon," Betty pointed out, "and he hasn't tried anything yet. Besides, he helped carry those cases of hers and he gave her the keys himself. It's peculiar. Oh, Charles, do you suppose that—that it's *me* he's after?"

Before he could answer, a robot came in, a practical, old-fashioned model with four arms for waiting at table.

"Dinner is served." It snapped its aluminum jaws. "Come to the dining room, please."

Reluctantly, they obeyed.

"Whatever you do," whispered Charles warningly at the door, "don't let him ply you with liquor."

The captain stood at the head of the table. He was in full evening dress, with a heavy gold-nugget watch chain across his muscular middle. He smelled faintly of mothballs and looked very respectable.

The Buttons examined the table. There wasn't a sign of absinthe or brandy or even champagne. There was nothing but water.

"It's too bad your cousin won't join us," said the captain, seating them courteously. "I hope those cartons of hers have something tasty inside them."

"They contain Dr. Stringfellow's Vegetable Remedy and Tonic for Gentlewomen," replied Betty primly. "It is said to be very nourishing."

Their host shuddered. Recovering, he clapped his hands sharply. "Oh, steward!"

"Aye, aye, sir!" said the robot, appearing with a big silver tureen and setting it down on the table.

The Buttons drew back.

"I can see you don't trust me," laughed the captain. "So we'll serve everything out in plain sight. You can shuffle the plates if you want to." He proceeded to ladle out a clear, fragrant soup. "There. Take whichever you want."

The Buttons selected their plates. They picked up their spoons, dipped them nervously, made rowing motions.

The captain ate heartily, talking away between spoonfuls. He told them that Sugar Plum was surrounded by an ionized layer impervious to DoItAll waves. He said he had no use for such gadgets, or for the Age which produced them.

"And why," he demanded, "did we become fake Victorians? Why are we worse than the real ones? I'll tell you. Because space was too big. It made people feel puny. They wanted a hole to crawl into—something small, safe and stuffy."

As course followed course, he told them how he had retired from piracy after homesteading Sugar Plum. Alone with his robots, he had dismantled his vessel, using its engines for heating and lighting. He had done a good deal of exploring.

The robot served something like lobster, and something like grouse, and a roast which might have been venison. It served vegetables in pink, pear-like clusters and long, golden pods. It served a crisp, succulent salad.

Charles picked at his food, watching Betty with growing uneasiness. First, her appetite seemed to improve. Then her eyes started to sparkle, and the severe little corners of her mouth began to relax. Leaning forward intently, she became more and more absorbed in the captain.

"—and so here I've been ever since," he said, as he finished his salad, "and Sugar Plum's just about perfect. Of course, it gets lonely at times, but—"

Abruptly, Betty's hand darted out, grabbed the captain's beard.

"*Beaver!*" she shouted, laughing and pulling. Then she settled back, blushing. "I've wanted to do that for years."

Charles reeled. Here was a crisis! He started to rise; hesitated. Of course, he was shocked to the core, but, "Great Scott, she's pretty!" he thought; and at once he felt guilty.

He stood up, trying hard to look angry.

"Elizabeth," he announced, "you will leave this room—er—instantly."

"Why?" giggled Betty.

"Because *ladies* do not pull gentlemen's beards."

The captain was holding his sides and rocking with laughter.

"Now, now," he protested. "Let her get it out of her system. 'Beaver's' a splendid old custom. It's almost Victorian."

Betty dimpled, resting her chin on the backs of her interlaced hands. "Don't pay any attention, Captain Burgee. Charlie's a horrid old fuss-pot. Why shouldn't I yank at your beard? I like you."

"Betty, the man is a *pirate*!"

"Not any more. He's retired. You heard him say so yourself. Anyhow, I like him. I think he'd make an awfully nice husband for Cousin Aurelia."

Charles reached for the water, and drained his glass in a spluttering gulp.

"I think so, too," the captain agreed, looking pleased. "I thought so as soon as I saw her. She's exactly my type." He sighed. "But she does seem a little unfriendly. Do you suppose a guitar and some old-fashioned songs at her window might—well, make her want to get better acquainted?"

Charles thought, "Not that sour old prune!" Surprised at himself, he swallowed the words just in time.

Betty snickered. "Poor Cousin Aurelia! I simply can't get over her staying locked in with nothing but Vegetable Remedy. Why, it tastes just like shoe polish. And it's all because she's scared to death to eat or drink anything here. She believes that Sugar Plum's really an—an uninhibited planet!"

She stopped. She stared at the captain. "What's the matter?"

"I'm afraid," he said, looking very serious, "that you don't understand. Your Cousin Aurelia is right."

Betty wilted. "You can't mean it!"

"I don't know exactly what does it. Maybe it's something in the water and air and food—"

Charles stared at the plates on the table in horror.

"It's nothing you need be afraid of," the captain went on. "You see, its effect just depends on the kind of person you are way inside."

Betty began to perk up. She eyed Charles appraisingly.

"Is Charles the right kind of person?" she asked.

"I'm sure he is, and your cousin is, too, though she keeps it pretty well hidden. If they weren't, Sugar Plum would soon let us know it, believe me." He grinned. "And now let's all go a-courtin'. I'll get my guitar and call Herman."

He went to the door and whistled, and instantly a large reddish creature came lolloping in. It saw the guitar and blinked eagerly.

Betty linked her arm in the captain's. "Come along, Charlie."

Charles fumbled around. He was scared.

Then Betty looked over her shoulder and smiled. It was a completely new smile. He had never seen it before. It made him tremble with apprehension.

"You know," she said softly, "I think it'll sort of be fun being uninhibited."

Charles knocked over a glass, and his chair, and he paused only to drink some more water.

"So," he shouted, "do I!"

"I suspected you might," said the captain.

Together they went out on the porch and sat down in a swing; and, for a few moments, in silence, they watched Sugar Plum's two moons sailing through the strange, perfumed sky. The larger was celadon green; the smaller, off-white, was glowing, gleaming.

Finally, "Cousin Aurelia?" called Betty.

"Betty, are you out in the dark with that man?"

"Charles and I both are. But he isn't a pirate any more and he's really quite nice. Besides, he's going to sing to you."

"You tell him to go away—far away. I've barricaded the window and I have my sharp scissors. I warn you, if he makes one false move—"

"This is where I came in," remarked Charles.

The captain settled back, tuned his guitar, and started to sing in a warm bass-baritone, with Herman whistling a tenor obbligato through his nose.

Betty and Charles thought the effect was charming, even if Herman did tend to go a bit flat on the high notes.

First, the captain sang *Down by the Old Mill Stream* and *Sweet Genevieve*. Then he tried a number of sentimental arias from the more respectable operas, and *The Lost Chord*, and several other old favorites.

Occasionally, Cousin Aurelia sniffed loudly, but she said nothing until his serenade came to an end.

"Betty!" she called. "Can you hear me?"

"Do I have to?"

"Tell that person out there that it has done him no good to make those ungodly noises. My fingers have been in my ears all the time."

"You must've been really a sight," giggled Betty.

"Betty! You—you sound different, somehow."

"Oh, I am! So is Charles. We're both uninhibited now."

There was one cry of horror from Cousin Aurelia and then silence.

Betty turned to the captain. He looked downcast, and Herman did, too.

"We'll just have to try something else, something clever," she told the captain. "Cousin Aurelia seems dead set against you. It's because of your being a pirate, I guess."

Charles and Betty spent the next couple of days avoiding any mention of the captain's former profession and helping him think up new ways to uninhibit Cousin Aurelia. He tried singing again, this time with an augmented chorus of Herman's relations. When that also failed, he cooked her a fine mushroom omelette. Then he caught her a young animal with lavender ears to keep as a pet and he spent a whole evening reading *Sonnets from the Portuguese* aloud at her window.

She responded with sniffs and with occasional scraping noises of furniture being moved to reinforce her defenses. Finally, to Betty's distress, she pushed out a note announcing that henceforth she would have nothing to do with the Buttons—and that no one could tell her that poems like those were *Victorian.*

Before the third day was half over, the Captain was moping around, Charles was peevish, and Betty had started to worry and fret.

So, in the late afternoon, they went on a picnic. Followed by Herman, and by the four-armed dining room robot carrying two wicker hampers, they walked around the lake to a broad grassy knoll where the strange square trees grew in a circle, and prisms of quartz leaned from the ground like Druids turned into stone. While they ate, the night advanced softly, its moons weaving crystalline shadows of celadon, rose, and old ivory.

Betty waited until the last hint of daylight had vanished. Then, "It's lovely," she whispered. "Poor Cousin Aurelia, it'd all be so simple if she'd only come out, but—oh, I'm afraid that it's hopeless!"

"Hopeless?" Charles snorted. "It's easy. We'll break into her room, me and Burgee, and hold her while you pour some of Sugar Plum's water down her gullet. She'll be fixed up before she finds out what hit her."

"We mustn't do that," the captain said stiffly. "We can't employ violence."

"Look who's talking!" Charles was amused. "An old pirate like you. Robbing ships, making passengers walk the plank into space, shooting people with ray guns, and—"

"Shh!" Betty warned. "Charles, that isn't polite. You know he's sensitive about—"

The captain seemed to be strangling. "And I thought it was *snobbery*!" Then he exploded with laughter. He lay back on the grass and he howled.

The Buttons stared in amazement, and some creatures came out of the trees to see what the uproar was all about.

The captain sat up. "What century is this?" he asked.

"The Twenty-second, of course," answered Betty. "But—but why?"

"I just wondered. I'll tell you later." He controlled himself with an effort. "But we really mustn't use force on Aurelia, even in such a good cause. It might turn her into the wrong kind of person."

"Turn her?" Betty repeated sadly. "I'm afraid that she already is. I don't think she'll ever come out. I'm afraid she'll do something desperate."

"I'm worried, too," the captain admitted, "but I'm certain she is the right kind. The wrong kind of people can't live here. Sugar Plum doesn't like them."

Betty and Charles both looked puzzled.

"I'll try to explain. It happens within a few hours, even if they aren't uninhibited. If they are, then it's practically instantaneous. It's a—"

He broke off and looked up at the sky with a frown. There was an angry red glow right above them, a far-distant roar.

They leaped to their feet. The glow brightened swiftly. It seemed to be headed straight for them. The sound filled the air.

"We have visitors!" shouted the captain.

"Wh-who?" stammered Betty. "The police?"

"They don't use braking jets any more. It's an obsolete freighter."

"Oh!" Betty put her hands to her face in terror. "It's the *Beautiful Joe*. That man Possett—he's coming back after Cousin Aurelia!"

The red glow passed to the northward. They saw the ship's shape for a moment, spurting flame, slowing. Then it dropped out of sight. The ground shuddered briefly. There was quiet.

The captain grabbed Betty's arm. "They're down in the clearing. Quick! When he dropped you, did Possett take anything with him?"

"Just a fresh supply of water."

"My God!" blurted Charles. "That means they're—"

"*Uninhibited!*" yelled the captain. "And they're the wrong kind of people. Betty! Charles! Can you run? Hey, Steward, give them a hand!"

"Aye, aye, sir," snapped the robot, hoisting the hampers and reaching an elbow to each of the Buttons.

"Then let's go. I hope we can make it in time to save them!"

"*Them?*" gulped Charles, as the robot started to run.

But the captain already was too far ahead to have heard him.

Pulled by the untiring robot, Charles and Betty made very good time, but they couldn't catch up with the captain. They had to make several stops to get their wind back, and they were still half a mile from the house when they heard her.

"Help! Murder! Police! Save me!" screamed Cousin Aurelia.

"He—he's got her!" puffed Charles, as the shrieks died away. "Hurry!"

When they got to the house, it was empty. Not even Herman was there. In the living room and the hall, there were signs of a titanic struggle. The door of Cousin Aurelia's room hung wide open.

"Look!" Charles gave it a great goldfish stare. "She unlocked it herself!"

"He probably told her—he was rescuing her—from the pirate," panted Betty.

"We—we'll have to go on—" Charles felt his legs start to collapse—"to the clearing."

The robot put two arms around him, and one around Betty.

"You will rest for three minutes," it stated, leading them to the living room and seating them gently. "I will bring brandy."

The brandy was welcome. They drank it in gulps, and worried about Cousin Aurelia, and the robot fanned them considerately while they did so.

Then, again, they were off. In less than ten minutes, they looked down on the valley, on the clearing. They caught sight of the *Beautiful Joe*. The voice of the waterfall reached them.

And so did another one. A man's voice. A deep one.

"Ow!" it yelled hoarsely. "Let me up! Ow! Let go!"

Charles moaned. "We shouldn't have waited for brandy. Now they're killing him, too!"

With the robot behind them, they raced down the hill, splashed through the stream, broke through a circle of giggling Sugar Plum natives and goggle-eyed creatures.

"Don't give up!" croaked Charles. "We're coming!"

On the grass were four figures. Two were thrashing around and being sat on. Two were doing the sitting.

The Buttons braked to a stop. Something was radically wrong. The larger of the two thrashing figures was being sat on by Cousin Aurelia!

"Try to kidnap *me*, will you?" *Slap*. "Make me throw myself into that pool!" *Slap*. "And swallow a gallon of water and have to drag myself out!" *Slap-slap-slap*. "You will, will you?"

"Ow!" cried the figure. "Leg-go!"

Aurelia looked over her shoulder. She spied Charles and Betty.

"Hey!" she shouted. "Bear a hand here with Possett!"

"You don't have to hold him," called Captain Burgee, dismounting from Loopy the mate. "He can't get away. Sugar Plum's got him."

They both rose and the two writhing figures continued to writhe.

"They're *scratching*," Charles exclaimed.

He wasn't quite right. The skipper and the mate of the *Beautiful Joe* were trying to scratch, but they didn't have enough hands. They were groaning, and bleating, and begging for aid as they wriggled.

Cousin Aurelia gave Possett a push with her foot.

"I'm soaked to the skin," she announced. "Betty, help me off with this dress. If I don't wring my petticoat out, I'll catch something."

"Why, Cousin Aurelia!" Charles blurted. "In front of the captain?"

"And why not?" she demanded. "I have undies on, don't I?"

The captain broke in, his voice urgent. "We've got to get these characters back aboard in a hurry! They can't live on Sugar Plum; they're the wrong kind of people. I started to tell you. They're allergic to the critters, the trees, the natives—to everything here. You, Steward!" He beckoned. "Call the crew of the *Beautiful Joe*."

The robot ran to the ship. It whistled. Immediately, four other robots appeared.

"Bosun," said the captain to the one in the lead, "Captain Possett is ill. He is—er—delirious. The mate, too. Carry them in. And take off quickly for New Texas."

"Aye, aye, sir." The bosun saluted.

They lifted up Possett, who was grunting and swearing. They hoisted the weasel-faced mate. The hatches clanged shut. Fire burst from the stern. The ship lifted.

When there was quiet again, Cousin Aurelia looked at the captain. She examined him carefully.

"Hm-m-m," she murmured to Betty. "Not bad. Not bad at all!"

Then, "Alexander Burgee," she declared, "every bit of this is your fault. If I hadn't escaped from that man and jumped in the pool—well, I don't know *what* might've happened. The least you can do is carry me back to your house."

At midnight, Charles and Betty sat in the living room. They hadn't had time to get used to the change in Cousin Aurelia and they still looked at her unbelievingly. She was wearing a gay housecoat of Betty's, too tight in just the right places. She had let down her hair, tied it with a ribbon, and she'd put on a gay smear of lipstick. She was exceedingly merry.

"I can't imagine how I stood it," she was saying, "for so many years. I mean, being such an old frump." She laughed brightly. "Why, I was almost as bad as poor Charlie!"

"Well, at least I never locked myself in to get away from a pirate," Charles retorted.

The captain stood up with a chuckle. "Say, that reminds me." He went to a bookcase, opened a thick volume, and gave it to Charles. "I want you to read something here."

Charles saw that it was *Jane's Dictionary of Space Transportation*. He looked up enquiringly.

The captain was pointing at a word.

"'*Pirate*,'" Charles read, sounding puzzled. "'Pirate, originally a criminal who attacked and robbed ships at sea (see: Earth, planet) now obsolete in this sense. At present, term applied to—'" Charles hesitated—"'to persons engaged in space salvage, especially to captains of vessels employed in such work.'"

Charles turned red. Betty flushed. Cousin Aurelia started laughing her head off.

"Times change," the captain said soberly. "Do you want me to show you my license?"

The Buttons were much too embarrassed to answer.

"Well, if you don't, I hope you'll excuse us. Aurelia and I would like to sit in the swing and look at the stars for a while."

"I want to be told just how far away Boston is," she said as he helped her to rise. She wrinkled her nose. "I'm certainly glad that here on Sugar Plum we're safe from the wrong kind of people—all those horrible Victorians."

The captain's arm went around her.

He winked at the Buttons.

"A few of them weren't so bad," he said gently. "A few of the real ones."

And, as they left, he slipped the copy of *Sonnets from the Portuguese* into his pocket.

"Well, now that we've sort of lost Cousin Aurelia," said Betty, "I wish I could have one of these adorable animals on Sugar Plum for my very own. As a pet, you know. It might help as a substitute for Cousin Aurelia's company."

"And what's wrong with me for a substitute?" Charles wanted to know. "It seems to me that you can forget Cousin Aurelia for a change and give me a little consideration."

She looked at him appraisingly and then at her watch.

"I never thought of that," she said. "It's time for bed."

Later, she sat up, studied him hard for a moment, and shook her head wistfully.

"Oh, Charles, you'd be perfect," she said, "if you only had lavender ears."

"That shouldn't be much trouble," he answered gravely. "I'll signal a passing spaceship, get to New Texas and have my ears tattooed. Good enough?"

She nuzzled against his neck.

"Wonderful, darling. It would make you look so—so Bohemian!"

It was the finest compliment Charles had ever received.

www.ingramcontent.com/pod-product-compliance
Ingram Content Group UK Ltd.
Pitfield, Milton Keynes, MK11 3LW, UK
UKHW042152281224
453045UK00004B/364